STAT

DOUBLE TEAM

by AMAR'E STOUDEMIRE
illustrated by TIM JESSELL

SCHOLASTIC INC.

To my family, my mother, and Hazell.
You are my inspirations.

*   *   *

Special thanks to Michael Northrop

ISBN 978-0-545-38760-6

Cover and interior art by Tim Jessell
Original cover design by Yaffa Jaskoll

12 11 10 9 8 7 6 5 4 3 2 1   12 13 14 15 16 17/0

Printed in the U.S.A.   40

First printing, October 2012

I knew this move so well that I was on autopilot as soon as I took that first step. I made a quick shift to my right, rose up as high as I could, and . . . put my socks away in the top drawer. The clean ones anyway. The dirty ones went in the laundry basket, over a layer of underwear and other stuff that definitely needed to be covered up.

It was Saturday morning. I'd just gotten back to Lake Wales the night before, too late to worry about this kind of stuff. Now I was moving around my room, putting stuff away and checking for any signs that Dad had been poking through my things while I was gone. I didn't expect to find any. Pops trusted me, and I trusted him.

I wasn't as sure about Junior. We were tight, but I'd caught him playing one of my video games or scuffing up a new ball of mine more than once. I didn't have to worry about that this time because he had gone on the trip with me. We had gone to visit our mom and our half brother, up in New York.

It was always nice to see Mom — I missed her a lot — and my little bro was getting so big. He was a little man now! But it was nice to be back in my hometown of Florida, too. I walked around my bed and over to my desk, sorting through the books in my hands instead of looking where I was going. I didn't need to look: Everything was just where I left it.

I heard three loud knocks on the front door just as I was hanging up my new shirt that I had bought in New York. I knew that sound. It was my friend Mike, rapping on the side of the door. Before I even reached the kitchen, I knew Deuce would be standing next to him. I opened the door and sure enough, there they were.

"Hey, Amar'e," said Mike.

"Change into some shorts," said Deuce. "We need to practice!"

He was holding a basketball, as usual. He dribbled it three quick times to make his point: *Bomp! Bomp! Bomp!*

"What," I said, "no hello?"

I was just joking. The sound of the ball bouncing on the walkway was all the hello I needed. I let them into the kitchen while I went to change into shorts and sneakers and get my ball. I'd missed playing ball with my friends while I was away. Junior and I hit the courts a few times, but our half brother was still really young. When Mom said, "Why don't you play some hoops with your little brother?" she really meant "Why don't you watch him while I go to the supermarket?"

I got the shorts out of the laundry pile because I was just going to sweat them up anyway.

We left the house and started walking toward our regular court, in the little town park near my house.

"House was pretty quiet. Was your dad home?" Deuce asked.

"Nah," I said. "It's his busiest time of year at work. He's hardly home at all. That's why it was a good time to visit New York."

"'Bout your bro?" said Mike.

"Already at work," I said. "He's got a job now, weekends and after school. Think he's saving up for a new car."

"That's cool. Too bad he won't have it in time for next weekend," Deuce said.

"Why's that?" I asked.

"He could drive us to the next tournament," said Deuce.

"There's another tourney?" I said.

"Yeah," said Mike. "And we might've, you know, gone ahead and signed you up."

"We didn't think you'd mind," said Deuce.

"Safe bet," I said.

We took all the hometown shortcuts and reached the court in no time flat. We had the place to ourselves when we got there, so we spread out and took our time warming up. The hoop on one end of the court was bent, so I turned and headed toward the other one.

"Take the shot!" called Mike.

He didn't have a ball. He was waiting for one of us to shoot so he could swoop in and scoop up the rebound. I took a few more dribbles and picked up my pace. Then

I rose up and launched a fadeaway jumper, pretending someone was on me tight. "Swish!"

"Let's work on pick-and-rolls," said Deuce.

That was my favorite move.

"You guys remember when Carlos and his crew tried to take over this court?" I said.

A few weeks ago, some older guys had come around and tried to kick us off our own home court. We played a big game to see who'd get to stay.

"'Course!" said Mike. "We wouldn't have won if it wasn't for that pick-and-roll you two pulled off at the end."

"Yeah, that was sweet," said Deuce. "But we need to keep working. These tourney teams can definitely play some D. And the one this weekend is the toughest yet."

"I'm on it," I said.

"Yeah, right," said Deuce, doing a quick, slick crossover dribble as he talked. "You barely even signed up for that first tournament."

"Yeah, and who was MVP of the last one?" I shot back.

I had him there. But Deuce was right, too. The teams we were playing now definitely knew their stuff.

Whatever play we ran, they'd seen it before. And it sounded like the teams this weekend were going to be even better.

"All right, let's do this!" I said, clapping my hands twice.

"Hold up, hold up," Mike said.

I saw another kid edging onto the court. Deuce held the ball and we all turned toward this guy. He looked familiar. He was tall and thin and had a little forward lean to him, like a bendy straw. Then I remembered where I'd seen him. He was the new kid in our grade at school.

"Hey, Doug-AY!" called Mike.

Yeah, that was his name: Dougie. Deuce gave him a little wave and he waved back. Then he headed over to where we were standing near the free throw line.

He had this complicated handshake that was like: bump fists, hook fingertips together, up tap, down tap, and another fist bump. I was surprised when Mike and Deuce both knew it. He turned to me last. His hand was out, ready for the fist bump, but I just nodded. I hadn't caught all of the parts to their handshake, and anyway that wasn't the kind of move I came here to work on.

Mike must've figured out what I was thinking because he said, "Dougie's been practicing with us while you were away. He's a good guy."

"Cool," I said. "I'm Amar'e."

"I know," he said. "I'm Dougie."

"I know," I said. We both smiled, but I still didn't shake his hand. I wasn't being mean: I still had no idea of the order!

Anyway, there were four of us now. I thought we should keep working on the pick-and-roll, with defenders on both players like in a real game. It got even more complicated with all that traffic coming together at one spot. But they all wanted to run two-on-two right away.

"Yeah, come on, STAT," said Deuce. "We worked on all that stuff the whole time you were gone."

That didn't help me much, I wanted to say, but I didn't mind playing two-on-two. I kind of wanted to see what Dougie could do other than bump fists. I'd get a close look, too, because he wound up being my teammate.

"He's a pretty good distributor," said Deuce, meaning he was a guard.

"All right," I said. "We get the ball first."

"Why do they call you STAT?" Dougie asked as we waited for Mike and Deuce to line up and check the ball back to us.

"It's kind of a nickname," I said. "My dad gave it to me. It means Standing Tall and Talented. It's, like, part nickname and part reminder."

"Cool," he said.

Dougie played with the same forward lean he had when he walked. His head was always a little in front of his body. It made him look kind of like he was trying to read an eye chart, but it gave him a wicked head fake. Deuce bit on one right off the bat, and Dougie snuck by him and laid it in to give us an early lead.

We were playing make it, take it, because the trash talk was better that way, and I scored the next bucket. I got decent position down low. Then Dougie bounced the ball to me and I worked Mike over with a quick up-and-under move. It was harder than usual because of Mike's new size. He'd grown a lot in the last few months, though most of it was sideways. Just like that, we were up 2–0.

It was a pretty good game after that. Mike and Deuce pulled out all the stuff they'd been working on while I was gone — and Deuce stopped biting on that head fake. So the game got better, but the outcome didn't change. That two-point lead grew to three and then four. We didn't even know what we were playing to, but we knew where this one was headed.

After a while, I drained a jumper to make it 8–4. It was a fadeaway jumper that I didn't even need to fade away on: Mike wasn't on me that tight to begin with.

"Too easy," I said. And no offense to anyone — Mike and Deuce were my best friends, and they played hard — this is just the way we talked when we played.

"Let's switch 'em up after this," said Deuce.

"Sure," I said, but I knew it wouldn't matter.

It wasn't 8–4 because of Dougie. He was all right, but he was kind of an in-between player. He was a little slow for a guard and pretty skinny for anything else. I guess being away for a week made it a little easier for me to see what was going on. Yeah, we were all getting better. We could run pick-and-rolls and baseline screens and half a dozen other things. But I was getting, well, *betterer*. That wasn't a real word, but it was still a fact.

Dougie and I ran a pick-and-roll of our own that forced our defenders to switch off. Mike was covering Dougie now: no real advantage there. But Deuce didn't have the height to cover me. I rose up and drained a jump shot I didn't even need to jump on.

"Gonna let anyone else score?" Mike said.

And from the way he said it, I knew it wasn't just trash talk. He had meant it.

CHAPTER 2

We played until late afternoon. We were all wiped out by then, and I needed to get home and eat lunch. Things had gotten tense during the game. Sometimes that happens, even if it's just because of a foul or something. I wasn't too worried. Mike, Deuce, and I had been friends for a long time — and a lot of games. In the past, we'd always been good at shaking it off.

Right now, I needed to shake off this hunger. I was starving! I kept picturing my fridge, trying to remember what was in there and decide what I'd eat first. The more I thought about it, the faster I walked. Then I remembered a slice of pie I'd seen on the bottom shelf. If I didn't get home soon, I'd drool all over myself.

And then I got home and forgot all about it. Dad's truck was in the driveway. I'd barely seen him since I'd been back, just a little the night before. I pushed through the door, and there he was, sitting at the kitchen table. He had a fork in his hand and a little plate in front of him with some plastic wrap balled up off to the side.

"Aw, man, Pops," I said. "I was going to eat that!"

"Eat what?" he said, scooping up the last bite of pie and popping it into his mouth. "Still plenty of food in there, anyhow."

I made a move toward the fridge, but he was too fast: "Wash up first!" he said.

Man, I really needed to work on my first step.

When I got back, my hands were cleaner than Dad's plate. But the pie wasn't the only thing that was wiped out. Dad was slumped back in his chair. He still had his work clothes on, the sleeves rolled up on his green shirt.

"You done for the day?" I asked as I pulled a plate down from the cupboard above the sink.

"Nope," he said, letting out a long, slow breath. "Got another job in about" — he looked down at his watch — "about right now."

Dad had his own lawn-care company, and Saturdays were always his busiest days. A while ago, we saw a sign over in Lakeland that said SMALL BUSINESS SATURDAY. We both laughed: Every Saturday was Small Business Saturday when you owned a lawn-care company. The main reason was that Dad's customers liked to be home to "help out." From what I'd seen, that consisted of about 20 percent telling Dad and his guys what needed doing and about 80 percent getting in the way and nitpicking. That made the long hours a little longer.

Dad looked down at the empty plate and gave himself a few more seconds. Then he took a deep breath and stood up. "See you tonight," he said.

"Okay, Dad," I said. "Don't forget to give 'em the bill."

"I never do!" he said on his way out the door.

I heard his truck start up as I was leaning into the fridge and filling up my plate. I heard it pull out as I sat down. I looked over at his empty chair, and I was really glad he got that last slice of pie.

• • •

I was back in school on Monday. I'd missed time the week before, but I still had to keep up with the assignments.

Deuce was a really good student, too, and he let me know about the reading and homework and all that over the phone. And Mom did the rest. I'd have one foot out the door, and she'd turn me right around with a quick "You finished that homework, right?"

Most of it I didn't mind, like history. I really liked history. And English, too, because I've always liked reading. Sometimes the assignments were less fun, but it didn't matter. Mom made sure I did them all, just like Dad did when I was home.

Anyway, every class I went to, I handed in a thick stack of homework first thing. Most of my teachers were happy I'd done it, but I think a few of them were annoyed because now they had to grade it all. Especially our science teacher, Mr. Norris. He got a really sour look on his face when I handed in my work. I wanted to say: "Hey, if you just give me all A's, you won't have to sweat it." But I didn't. We called Mr. Norris "Mr. Bore-us" because he had zero sense of humor.

Anyway, I sat with the usual crew at lunch: Mike and Deuce, plus our friends Tavoris and Marcus. They spent the whole time catching me up on what had happened while I was away. Dougie joined us, too. He was actually standing there for a while before we saw him.

"Come on down," I said once I noticed him hovering over us. We scooted over and made some space. He didn't have much to say, though. I guess he was still getting to know everybody.

He did say one interesting thing, right before the bell: "You guys ready for the tournament?"

Mike, Deuce, and I all answered at the same time.

"Sure," I said.

"Maybe," said Deuce.

"Think so," said Mike.

"You need to get your story straight!" said Marcus.

"What we need to do is practice," said Mike.

"Can't today," said Deuce. "How about tomorrow?"

"Sure," I said.

"No problem," said Mike.

"You should sign up, too," Deuce said to Dougie.

"Yeah," I said.

He just shrugged: "It's three-on-three."

"What about these two?" I said, nodding over at Tavoris and Marcus.

"Don't look at me," said Marcus. "I just talk a good game."

We all laughed at that, too: He was the biggest motormouth in the whole grade.

No one was home after school. Dad's truck was long gone, and Junior's beat-up old car was nowhere in sight. I didn't have a car, but I had my Mongoose bike. I loved to skateboard, but is there anything better than the speed of a bike? It can't go as far or as fast as a car, but it never gets stuck in traffic. Anyway, it was another nice day in Polk County, so I decided to take it for a spin.

What I liked best about riding my bike was just thinking. I could go anywhere I wanted. Well, not Miami or anything, but anywhere in town. And I could just be by myself and think.

I thought about something else. Deuce couldn't play today, but Mike could. Used to be, the two of us would hit the court on our own. This was before the tournaments, before the practices. We'd go there just for fun and maybe some one-on-one. This time, neither of us had even mentioned it.

I kept pedaling. I had a lot to think about.

CHAPTER 3

*T*he rest of the week zipped by. It usually did when I was catching up on stuff. Pretty soon it was Saturday morning: tourney time! This one was called the High Flyer 3-on-3, and the signs all said: A CONTEST OF WILLS AND A BATTLE OF SKILLS. That sounded good to me!

"Check this out," said Deuce, pointing to one of the signs. "I wonder how we *will* do. *Will* we win?"

"That's not what they mean by 'a contest of wills,' you nerd," said Mike.

"Yeah, and you're not what they mean by 'skills'!" said Deuce.

We were all in a good mood. The next practice had gone better than that first one. Dougie wasn't there, so we couldn't play two-on-two and mostly just worked on plays. We'd been running a lot of baseline stuff that we were sure would work here today, and our plays were looking pretty sharp.

We'd arrived a little early because my dad had dropped us off on his way to work. We'd already signed in and stretched out. "We should check out the rims," I said.

"Yeah, I'm going for an eagle-eye view," said Mike, raising the ball above his head like he was getting ready to throw down a monster two-handed jam.

"Well, it is called the High Flyer," I said.

"Bet you a dollar you don't," said Deuce. At his height, Mike had no shot at dunking. Betting against us was his way of joining in.

"You're on!" said Mike.

Long story short: We owed Deuce a buck. Mike and I each took three tries at dunking. If it didn't happen on the first few, it pretty much wasn't going to happen. And we didn't want to tire out our legs before the tournament even started. (Of course, if Deuce had bet us *five* bucks, we would've been trying till sundown!)

I got really close on my second attempt. I tried it one-handed. I could extend a little more that way, but holding on was trickier. I had big hands for an eleven-year-old, but still. Anyway, I started with a flat-out sprint, at least ten feet, not even pretending to dribble. Then I launched myself up at the rim. I brought my hand back. The ball wobbled a little, but I held on tight. At the absolute top of my jump, I slammed it forward.

The ball hit the rim, but it shot straight up in the air. That meant the bottom of the ball had hit the top of the rim. I was definitely getting close to dunking — and I was still growing pretty fast. Before I even landed I thought: *I'll get there soon.*

Mike banged his shots off the rim a few times, but his bounced straight back. He was still growing, too, but he was kind of growing in both directions. He took off like a big old jetliner.

"Look out below!" I yelled after his last attempt, because he landed like a jetliner, too.

The other kids started to show up. Most of them just took lazy jumpers and stuff. That way, if they missed, they could act like they weren't really trying anyway. Some of them talked quietly because they knew people were listening. Some of them talked loudly for the same reason. I got a kick out of the loud ones.

We were watching this one loud, lanky kid strut around the court. He had bright yellow sneakers on that looked like hyperactive bananas when he moved. He rattled in a ten-foot shot and looked all around to make sure everyone saw it.

"What's he want, a prize?" said Mike.

"Maybe he should try not to use every inch of the rim next time," I said.

"No need to go bananas," said Deuce, as the kid chest-bumped one of his teammates.

And then all of a sudden, the court was empty.

"Are we starting up?" said Mike.

"Still too early," said Deuce.

It reminded me of this show I'd seen during Shark Week on TV. One minute, there were all these seals playing around and doing loop-de-loops in the water. The next second they just vanished. Then the camera started panning around, because the guy holding it knew the deal. A shark had showed up and scared off all the seals.

And now I saw the shark. He was long and lean like the cocky kid in banana shoes, but he wasn't strutting. He was just walking, nice and easy. And he wasn't looking around either. It was like he didn't care if people were watching or not.

"Check out this guy," I said.

"What do you mean," said Deuce, "good or bad?"

He hadn't done anything more than dribble the ball with his right hand yet, but I knew.

"Good," I said.

"How can you tell?" Deuce asked, but just then, the kid took off toward the basket. Three quick dribbles and he was there. Then he shot straight up and threw down a no-doubt-about-it, rim-rattling dunk. He used one hand, but it wasn't because he needed that extra inch.

"Whoa," I said.

There was a kid the next row down from us in the stands. He had a basketball in his hand, but I didn't see any teammates.

"Hey, man," I said.

"Yeah?" he said, looking back over his shoulder.

"Who's that guy?"

"That's Jammer, man," he said.

"Jammer?" said Mike.

"James 'Jammer' Jamison," said the kid. "He goes to my school."

"He your teammate?" I said.

"I wish."

"I think those are his teammates," said Deuce, pointing.

Two other kids had edged onto the court behind Jammer. The first one fired up a brick from twelve feet away. Jammer grabbed the ball and fired it to the other guy, who took a long shot that rattled around the rim and off. I was seriously relieved that his teammates weren't as good. But that only lasted the second or so it took Jammer to tip the miss up and in.

Fifteen minutes later, the first-round matchups were announced. We got Banana Shoes and two other kids. I'll admit, I was a little nervous before the game started. It wasn't that long ago that I had shied away from tournaments altogether. I'd always loved basketball, but I was still getting used to how serious these things were. Sometimes you'd see two teams play an entire game without any of the players cracking a smile, much less a joke. I didn't understand that at all.

Plus, the other team was strutting around the court like they owned it. Banana Shoes was their leader, or at least he was acting like he was. He looked over at us as we headed to center court for the opening tip. "This won't take long," he said, loud enough for us to hear it. He definitely talked a good game.

Yeah, that lasted about eighteen seconds. I won the tip cleanly, and batted the ball back to Deuce. My legs were moving even before I landed, like how they run in cartoons. The other team tried to keep up, but Deuce was too fast. He blew by them as they backpedaled. They turned to run after him and lost sight of me, trailing the play. Deuce just missed the layup. He was going about a hundred miles an hour, so it had a little too much on it. But I swooped in doing ninety-eight, for the easy tip-in.

Let's just say that their trash talk pretty much dried up after that. The games at this tourney were to eleven, scoring by ones. After we went up 7–3 on a nice up-and-under move from Mike, Banana Shoes started limping. Funny thing about that limp, though: It didn't affect him when he had the ball. He was just faking it, pretending that's the reason they were losing.

Anyway, we pretty much used the rest of the game as practice for the next one. Deuce did a good job of spreading the ball around, and when I got a rebound, I didn't necessarily go right back up with it. I looked to see if Mike had good position or if Deuce was cutting to the hoop or whatever. We won 11–5, and we all had about the same number of points. But I knew the day was just getting started.

CHAPTER 4

*M*y mouth was pretty dry after the game. There was a drinking fountain over by the sign-in table, and I headed straight toward it. I wanted to check if the second-round matchups were ready yet anyway. They weren't, but I drank about a gallon of cold water from the fountain.

I looked up and wiped my mouth with the back of my arm. There was a guy standing there. It was hard to tell how old he was because he was one of those old guys who was still in really good shape. He even looked kind of familiar, but I couldn't think where I'd seen him before.

"Here you go," I said, stepping aside so he could use the fountain.

"Thanks, son," he said, "but I'm fully hydrated."

Hydrated, that was a good word. I made a mental note to use it when I got back to the bleachers, like: "It's cool, I'm fully hydrated now."

"Your name's Amar'e, right?" the guy asked. He even pronounced it right.

"Yeah," I said, but he obviously knew that already. It's not like Amar'e is the first name you would guess. Anyway, he kept asking me questions.

"How old are you?"

"'Leven."

"Where you from?"

"Lake Wales."

"How tall are you?"

"Not sure. Keeps changing."

He took a step back and eyeballed me. I guess he was estimating my height. That's when it occurred to me, you know: *Why is this random dude asking me all these questions? And why am I answering?*

"Uh, who are you?" I said.

"Name's Omar," he said. He smiled and extended his hand.

He still looked kind of familiar. I didn't want to be rude, in case he was an old friend of Dad's or something. I shook his hand.

"Amar'e," I said, "but I guess we already covered that."

"Good luck next round," he said.

"Yeah, all right. Thanks."

I headed back to the bleachers. Mike and Deuce had their heads on a swivel, keeping an eye on two different games at once.

"Fully hydrated," I said, plunking down next to them.

"Fully what-what-ed?" said Mike.

"That's good," said Deuce. "Some of these other teams are tough."

"Yeah," said Mike. "I think they're fully hybraited, too."

"Hy*dra*ted, man," said Deuce with a chuckle.

By the time we explained what that meant to Mike, they'd started announcing the second-round match-ups. They announced ours for Court 2.

"They good?" I asked.

"Oh, yeah," said Deuce.

"Most def," said Mike.

We got up and headed down to Court 2 to find out just how good. We checked in with the ref once we got there, and the other team arrived about thirty seconds later. The first thing I noticed was that two of them were twins. They looked identical, and were wearing the same outfits, right down to their sneakers.

"This is gonna be confusing," said Mike.

Their third player didn't have a twin. Or if he did, he'd eaten him. Dude was enormous. Put it this way: The ball he was dribbling wasn't much rounder than he was.

"Is it still called 'boxing out' if the guy's round?" I whispered to Deuce.

He laughed, but it was kind of a nervous laugh. And he was right, too, because this game was tough from the start.

"You got him?" I called to Deuce as we got bounced around in traffic under the hoop.

"Got him!" called Deuce. But he covered the wrong twin. That left the other one wide open for a little bunny-hop layup.

"No, *him!*" I said as the ball went through the hoop.

"Oh, then no," said Deuce.

Mike didn't have to deal with mistaken identity. It was impossible to confuse the enormous kid he was covering with anything other than maybe a baby elephant. As big as he was, he never moved too far from the basket. From the start, the twins dumped the ball in to him on almost every play.

Sometimes he'd pass it back out, and sometimes he'd take it himself. Not only could I see it when he bodied up on Mike, I could hear it.

"OOOOOOF!" grunted Mike as the kid backed into him.

Before Mike could recover his position — or his breath — we were down 2–0. By the time I noticed that the twins had different color laces (in their identical sneakers), it was already 4–0.

"Red laces!" I called to Deuce. "See 'em?"

"Yeah," he answered. "Blue laces over here."

And that's how we identified them. At first, we called them "Red Laces," "Blue Laces," and "Big Man," but pretty soon we simplified things.

"Stay on Big!" Deuce called.

"I got Red," I shouted.

We got on the board after that with, well, with a little luck. I heaved up an off-balance jumper from long range and somehow it rattled in: 4–1. As we got ready for our next possession, I looked around at the matchups.

Big Man had a size advantage on Mike — he would've had a size advantage on a car! Mike was faster, but getting around Big Man was like Magellan trying to sail around the world. Deuce was a little faster than either twin, but a little smaller, too. And even if he got around his guy, Big Man would be right there, clogging up the lane.

I was the one with the best matchup. I was a little bigger than either twin, and at least as fast. We were already down by three. If we were going to win, I was going to have to carry the load.

I went to work. I had the ball and Red Laces was on me tight.

I gave him a quick crossover dribble and a little fake, then took off. I turned the corner on him and rocketed toward the basket. Big Man saw me coming, but he had to stay close to Mike under the basket. That left me plenty of space for a short, pull-up jumper. It was 4–2, and we just sort of chipped away at it after that.

With the score tied at 6–6, Deuce dumped the ball down to me. Blue wasn't on him that close, and he clapped his hands for a return pass. But I had good position and a few inches on Red. I went up with a hook shot and scored over the top of him. It gave us our first lead of the day, but Deuce wasn't happy.

"Come on, man, I was wide open," he said.

Deuce kept the ball on our next possession. He charged straight down the lane and crashed right into Big Man. With their size difference, it looked like a little kid running into the side of a bouncy castle. The ref whistled Deuce for an offensive foul, and the other team scored two straight to put us behind again.

We finally got the ball back. Blue was all over Deuce, and he finally passed me the ball. I had to work hard, but I got by Red again. I swooped in from the side, and Big Man left Mike to pick me up. Mike was open now, but he was really deep under the basket, just inches from the baseline. It didn't seem worth the risk, especially since I'd been knocking down these short jumpers all day.

I stopped, popped, and scored. It was 9–9, but now both of my teammates were mad at me.

"I'm working hard down there," said Mike. "Wouldn't kill you to get me the ball when I'm open."

"You were all the way under the basket," I said.

"That's a good thing!" he said.

"I'm just trying to win the game for us," I said.

"Oh, what, we're not?" said Deuce.

"No, I know," I said. "Of course you are."

What else could I say? How do you tell your best friends you don't think they can beat their defenders? Well, I guess I told them that by scoring the next two points. The first one was a put-back on a heave by Deuce, so they couldn't really blame me for that. But I scored game point on a long jumper from the corner. I just had a good feeling about it, so I took it.

Mike should've been happy it went in. I mean, (A) we won, and (B) Big Man had to stop leaning on him now. But when I went to high-five him, I thought he was going to leave me hanging. He finally raised his hand up and gave mine a weak slap.

"Supposed to be three-on-three," he said as he headed off the court.

I looked around for Deuce, but he was already gone. The only ones left were the guys on the other team. I shook their hands and we all agreed it was a good, tough game. They told me their real names, but they'll probably always be Red Laces, Blue Laces, and Big Man to me.

As I walked off the court to go find my teammates, I saw Omar still standing by the fence. He gave me a nod. I nodded back, but I still couldn't figure out why he looked so familiar.

CHAPTER 5

I picked up my pace to catch Mike and Deuce. "Two down, two to go," I said as I pulled even with them.

We'd made it through the first two rounds, so the next game would be the semifinal. If we won that one, we'd get to play in the championship game. So it was all good, but Mike and Deuce didn't even respond. Maybe they didn't hear me. More people had showed up as the morning went on, and it was kind of loud.

"Two to go," I repeated.

"We heard you," said Mike.

That was it: Three words and then they went back to the silent treatment. They were still mad.

"Come on," I said as we found a spot in the bleachers. "I had the best matchup. I had to push the action."

"Push the action?" said Deuce. "You mean hog the ball?"

"You guys both had the ball early," I said. "They were killing us."

"Oh, so you thought you'd just take things into your own hands?" said Mike.

I looked over at him. I didn't really know what to say. Because the answer was yes. That's exactly what I thought, and it's the only reason we ended up winning. We just looked at each other for a long second. Then I remembered something my dad said once: *If you don't know what to say, just say what you know.* "You couldn't get around that guy," I said.

Mike rolled his eyes. "Please," he said. "It just took me a little time to figure him out, is all."

"Yeah, okay," I said.

There was one of those weird pauses where both of us were waiting for the other one to say something more. We both thought we were right. I could either make things worse, or I could apologize. I manned up.

"My bad," I said.

Mike shook his head and looked away. But he didn't say anything else. So of course that's when Deuce decided to speak up.

"What about me?" he said.

I decided to do the same thing: Tell the truth and then apologize.

"You couldn't get any separation from your guy," I said. "But my bad anyway," I said.

"That's right," said Deuce.

It didn't make any sense. The two statements completely contradicted each other, but Deuce was agreeing to both. I think he just wanted to save some face. I think they both did. They didn't look as mad. Their jaws weren't clenched up like they were trying to crack a walnut anymore.

Down on the court, the last game of the morning was wrapping up. As I turned to look, one of the players flew toward the rim and slammed one down. It was that kid Jammer.

"Wow," I said.

Seeing him dunk when he was warming up was one thing. He had all the time — and steps — he needed for that. But doing it in a game was something else. He had to spot the opportunity and be ready for takeoff.

"Can't wait till I can do that," said Mike.

"Me neither," said Deuce.

Mike and I both looked at him. We smiled.

"Deuce, man," said Mike. "You're, like, five foot nothin'. That's going to be a long time from now. A very long time."

"No way," said Deuce. "I'm going to do it tonight."

At first he seemed serious. Then he broke out into a big smile, too: "As soon as I fall asleep and start dreaming!"

We all laughed. It felt good to laugh with my friends again. We settled in to watch the rest of the game. It was like sitting outside a chain-link fence at a construction zone and watching some heavy-duty demolition work. Jammer was the wrecking ball.

The other team just couldn't stop him. And he wasn't fighting for the ball either. His teammates were working hard to get it to him. I was going to say something about it, but I didn't. We were all getting along again, and they were watching the same game I was. I'm sure they saw what was going on. And I had something else to say anyway.

"See that guy by the fence?" I said, pointing to Omar.

"Yeah," said Deuce.

"Sure," said Mike.

"You know who he is?" I said.

"No, who?" said Mike.

"Nah, I don't know," I said. "I'm just asking. I think he was watching our game, too."

"The whole time?" said Deuce.

"Yeah, I'm pretty sure."

"Probably just a fan," said Mike.

"He looks pretty serious for a fan," I said. And it was true. He was watching the game like he was trying to memorize it, and he wasn't cheering or anything like that. He'd just nod every once in a while, like when Jammer made a really good play.

"Maybe he's an official or something," said Deuce. "He looks kind of familiar, though."

"Yeah, right?" I said. "That's what I was thinking."

"Yeah, well, I'm thinking your brother just arrived," said Mike, changing the subject.

"Junior's here?"

"Yeah," said Mike, pointing toward the parking lot. "Just pulled in."

I looked over. The first thing I saw was his familiar red car. Then I saw Junior unfolding his big frame from the driver's seat.

"Cool," I said. "He must've taken the afternoon off from his job to come watch us play." I leaned forward and started to stand up. It was game point down on the court, and Jammer was about to put the other team out of its misery. "You guys want to come say hi with me?"

The crowd cheered as Jammer's jumper went in. I smiled, pretending they were cheering because Junior had shown up. It was better than what that cheer really meant: Jammer's team had just advanced to the semifinals, too. We might have to play them.

"Nah," said Mike. "I'm starving and need to, like, 'hydrate' myself."

"Me too," said Deuce. "We'll probably run over to the store and grab some lunch."

We all headed down the bleachers. "Grab me something, okay?" I said as I veered off toward the parking lot. Mike said something, but I didn't catch it through the other people heading down out of the bleachers. I figured he'd just said yeah. We always grabbed food for each other. It was, like, standard procedure.

"What's up, STAT?" called Junior when he saw me. "You guys still in this?"

"You know it!" I said. "We're in the semifinals."

"Nice!" he said. "I was afraid I'd take the afternoon shift off and it would be all over by the time I got here."

"Give me some credit!" I said. "We had a scare last game, though. Other team had identical twins."

"No way!"

"Yeah, it was, like, double vision or something."

"How'd you stop 'em?" he asked. So I showed him. I even hammed it up a little and did some "live instant replays" of what went down. I didn't mention the thing with Mike and Deuce because I didn't want to bum him out. Plus, I sort of thought that had blown over. Basically

we just hung out and joked until I saw Mike and Deuce heading back from across the street.

"Okay, gonna go eat and get ready," I said.

"Cool, I'll grab some real estate in the bleachers," he said. "Good luck, little bro."

I appreciated the good wishes, but what I really needed was some food.

"Whatcha get me?" I said to Mike and Deuce, rubbing my hands together.

Their mouths were full with their own sandwiches, so I had to wait for the bad news.

"Nothing," said Mike, crumpling up his bag and draining a two-footer right into a trash can.

"Yeah, it didn't work out," said Deuce.

"What do you mean?" I said.

"I guess we just had a better matchup with the sandwich guy," said Deuce, balling up his empty bag and dunking it into the can.

"Now we're even," they said, walking by me.

Yeah, great. If we were all even, how come I was the only one whose stomach was rumbling?

CHAPTER 6

We were lined up at midcourt for the opening tip. The kid lined up across from me wasn't as tall as I was, but you never knew what kind of springs someone had until you saw them jump. The ref still wasn't ready, so I reached across and shook the kid's hand.

"Amar'e," I said.

"Joe," he said. "Good luck."

"Yeah, you too," I said. "But not too much!"

Jammer's team was in the other semifinal game, but these guys must've been good, too, to make it this far. We were about to find out how good. The ref threw the ball straight up and I won it cleanly, tipping it back to Deuce. That was our first highlight of the game, and for a while, it looked like it might be our last. Joe and his teammates could all shoot, handle the ball, and defend. They were really good at doubling down on whoever had the ball and forcing a turnover.

We got the ball, already down 4–2 in what felt like the blink of an eye. There was a problem with the game clock, and we huddled up while the ref was over at the scorer's table. "Man," I said, "we have got to stop falling behind early like this."

"Anyone see any weaknesses?" said Deuce. "Any, I don't know, anything?"

"I think I might have one," said Mike.

It was surprising because Mike would play until the sun went down, but he wasn't exactly known for breaking down the *X*'s and *O*'s.

"Yeah?" I said.

"The baseline is wide open," he said.

It's something we'd worked on at practice. I guess he noticed because he was down low most of the time.

"All right," I said. "Let's run something."

We broke the huddle with a plan in mind. We ran a little pick play along the baseline for Deuce, because he was the fastest and the smallest. He squeezed through the space between Mike and the end line. He had to tip-toe to stay in bounds. But when he came out the other side, he was wide open.

I was out by the free throw line to keep Joe too far away to help out, and in case Deuce needed to kick it out. He didn't. He laid it up and in for the easy score. It felt good to run a play we'd practiced, where we were all involved.

It didn't last. They closed up the baseline on our next possession. And Deuce's man blew by him on theirs. The first time he'd done that, I thought maybe it was a fluke. But, nope, his guy was faster than him. I hated that, because speed was Deuce's thing.

It was a big problem because he scored on him like four or five times. That's no joke when the game is to eleven. And it made Deuce really want the ball. I understood. I mean, if a guy keeps scoring on you, you want to score back. It's, like, a pride thing, and you need to have some pride on the court.

But if a guy is faster than you on offense, you can bet he'll be faster on defense, too. He kept cutting Deuce off and slapping at the ball and everything else. For a little guy, he was a big pain. Eventually, I had to start bringing the ball up the court as a point forward. And of course Deuce started calling for it right away.

Finally, it looked like he had some space so I gave it to him. Turnover. I tried to at least get Mike involved after that. He scored a few points down low, but it wasn't really enough.

It was a struggle to keep my energy up because I hadn't had any lunch. The more I thought about it, and the hungrier I got, the more that seemed like a dumb prank. And now I had to carry the load on an empty stomach.

I took it strong to the hoop on game point, mostly because I didn't think I had the energy to play much longer. I steamrolled Joe, and the ref probably could've called an offensive foul. He'd swallowed his whistle at about 9–9, though. I think he might've missed lunch, too.

No one shook hands when this one was over. We were in the finals, but I just headed straight off the court

and for the bleachers. I wanted to see if maybe Junior had some food in the car.

I spotted Junior in the second row. He had a good spot to watch the game and was giving me a thumbs-up. And then that dude Omar cut me off.

"Hey, Amar'e," he said.

"Hey, Omar," I said. But I was really thinking: *I don't know who you are, and I don't want to be rude, but I think my brother is eating a candy bar, and it won't last long.*

"Good game," said Omar.

"Thanks." I leaned to the left to look around him — he had some broad shoulders — and saw Junior's mouth moving. It was definitely a candy bar.

"You showed a little edge at the end there," he said.

"Uh-huh, okay," I said. I was pretty distracted.

"Even ran some point forward."

"Yeah. Point. Forward. Right."

Omar looked over his shoulder to try to see what I was looking at. "I guess I'll let you go," he said, taking a step to the side.

"Later," I said, zipping past.

By the time I got to Junior, the candy bar was only a memory and a wrapper.

"Got anything else?" I said.

"Might have half a sandwich left in the car."

"I'll take it!" I said.

Junior dug in his pocket for his keys. As I reached out to grab them, he said, "I saw you talking to Overtime. Pretty cool."

"To who?" I said, already picturing that sandwich.

"You know, Omar 'Overtime' Tanner," he said.

Holy Finger Roll! That's why Omar looked so familiar! Overtime was a hoops legend around here. I hit rewind on my brain. What had I said to him?

"I can't believe I just said 'Later' to Overtime Tanner!" I said.

Junior chuckled and said, "What did he want?"

I scanned the crowd but didn't see Overtime.

"You know what? I don't even know."

CHAPTER 7

I wolfed down the half sandwich. It was one of those piled-high deli deals, and it definitely hit the spot. Then I caught up with Mike and Deuce on my way back from the parking lot, and we headed over to the scorer's table to find out who we were playing in the championship game. We didn't even have to ask. Jammer's team arrived at the same time, wondering who they were playing.

We exchanged a round of "S'up?" and "Hey" with them. Everyone was trying to act cool. We'd seen them play, and they'd probably seen us play, too. But we didn't want to give anything away with our reactions.

"No surprise there," I said as soon as we walked away.

"Yeah, I wouldn't want to play a team that had beaten those guys anyway," said Mike.

"Uh, *we're* supposed to be that team," said Deuce.

"Oh, yeah."

"We got 'em," I said. "No problem."

What was I supposed to say? "Let's give up now"? But I definitely had my doubts. Jammer was legit, and they'd blown the other team away in the game we watched. And my team, well, we'd kind of battled through our games. Plus, as my dad would say, we weren't exactly firing on all cylinders.

"STAT, get me involved early this time," said Deuce.

He had a really serious look on his face, and I had to smile. He'd been more harm than help most of the day, but you had to love that confidence. It reminded me why we were friends, dumb pranks and missed shots and all. He must've been thinking the same thing, because he smiled back.

"I'll try, D," I said.

Some guy with a clipboard walked up to us and said, "Tip-off is in fifteen minutes, Court Number One."

I headed back over to Junior to let him know. Mike

and Deuce came with me, and it was kind of cool. We were in the finals, and pretty much everyone seemed to know it. People were pointing and whispering and sort of sizing us up as we walked by.

Jammer's team was good, but for the next fifteen minutes it was still 0–0. We had as good a shot as they did. And our chances were a thousand percent better than the teams that had already been eliminated — especially since *we'd* eliminated half of them.

We bumped into Big Man from that second team. He told us they'd made it to the third-place game, and he was on his way to meet up with the twins to get ready.

"Good luck out there," he said. I could tell he meant it. He wanted us to win because that would mean he'd been eliminated by the best team.

It felt good to know that people were pulling for us. The bad feelings from the last few games were fading away fast. Nothing cures hurt pride like feeling like you own the place, or at least half of it. And just before we reached the bleachers, we ran into someone else who had our back. Dougie had showed up to cheer us on.

"Sorry I'm late, had to do chores," he said.

"No problem, man," said Mike. "You're just in time."

"Yeah?" said Dougie, launching into that complicated handshake of his.

"Yeah," said Mike, matching him move for move. "We're in the finals!"

"Court One in, like, ten minutes," said Deuce, and he did the handshake, too.

What the heck? I thought, extending my hand. I tried to remember the sequence. It was, like, bump, up, down, finger-grab, and maybe a headstand in there somewhere. Dougie slowed it down a little, and I got it. You know, more or less.

"Go get 'em!" he said.

By the time we reached my big brother, we didn't really need to tell him anything. He already had a good view of Court 1, and he'd find out who we were playing once the game started up in five minutes. Dougie grabbed a seat next to him, and Mike and Deuce said hi. They hadn't seen him since before the trip to New York. Then we hustled over to the court to stretch out.

On the way, I saw Omar — I mean Overtime. He was at his usual spot, courtside. He nodded at me, and I

nodded back. I tried to get a little extra in my nod, like: *I know I nodded back before, but this time I know who you are.* But I'm not sure how much of that came through. There's only so much you can ask your chin to say.

Now that I knew who he was, it made me a little nervous to know he was watching. Deuce followed my eyes.

"That guy's back," he said.

"That's Overtime Tanner," I said.

"No way!" Deuce and Mike said at the same time.

"Yuh-huh," I said. "Heard he scored eighty points in a high-school game once."

"I heard it was a hundred," said Mike.

Jammer and his teammates were already on the court, just shooting lazy jumpers at one end. We headed down to the other end and shot a few of our own. We looked back over our shoulders and talked about how we'd match up with them. We didn't even need to say who had Jammer. I knew it was me. I swallowed hard and sank a fifteen-footer.

A few minutes later, we heard a whistle at midcourt. I wasn't the only one feeling some nerves, because Deuce just about jumped out of his sneakers on the first *tweet*.

"What? It was loud," he said.

We'd had this ref a few times already. He called a pretty good game. He was wearing a new ref's outfit that looked like it had just come out of the box. Even his shiny silver whistle looked new.

"That's one official-looking official," I said as we headed toward center court.

"Should we have changed or something?" said Mike, looking down at his sweaty, smudged T-shirt.

"They gave us these shirts," said Deuce. "If they wanted us to change, they would've given us new ones."

"Nah, this is good," I said. "No one's gonna want to defend you in that thing anyway!"

"All right, let's go," said the ref.

As soon as the joking stopped, the nerves set in. I lined up across from Jammer for the opening jump. I nodded at him and he nodded at me. This guy was pretty big up close. He bent his knees, and I bent mine. We were both coiled up like snakes ready to strike.

"You ready?" said the ref, the ball in his hand.

We both nodded without taking our eyes off the ball.

He threw it straight up into the afternoon sun.

CHAPTER 8

*F*our plays: That's all you need to know how the game went. The first happened right after Jammer won the opening tip. He didn't win it by much. Basically, it was the difference between being able to dunk and being able to slam the ball into the rim. Anyway, he tipped it back to a kid named Donyel.

We knew from the game we'd watched that this kid was their main ball handler. He was a little bigger than Deuce but it didn't look like he was as fast. Deuce was on him tight, but here's the thing: Donyel wasn't trying to score. He worked it around until he had a clean passing lane, then fired it in to Jammer.

Jammer gave me a good shoulder fake and then went up for the shot. He had just enough space. The ball cleared my fingers by about a centimeter, rolled around the rim, and dropped: 1–0.

Second play: Deuce took the ball up, and Mike and I battled for position. I finally got open and put my hands up for the ball. But Deuce decided to take it himself. He got around Donyel and rocketed toward the rim. Jammer saw him coming and left me to cut him off. I was thinking: *Good move, Deuce. Way to draw the defense.*

But instead of passing it to me now that I was open, Deuce went up with the shot. Jammer jumped to block it, but he didn't really need to. He wound up blocking it with his *elbow*.

"Come on, man, I was wide open," I said as we dropped back on defense.

"Yeah, that sounds familiar," he said. He'd said the same thing to me a bunch of times today.

Third play: They worked the ball down low to a kid named Dave. Mike was in good position, but he took his time and backed in toward the basket. I started shading over that way. He gave Mike a little shimmy and turned to his left with the ball. That was the side I was on, so I shot over to make the block.

But he didn't go up with it. He bounced it to Jammer — who I'd just left. And you can bet he went up with it: 2-0.

Fourth play: Deuce worked it into Mike down low. Now I'm thinking: *Okay, cool, we're going to run the same thing.* So I edge over toward him, but on offense now. If Jammer leaves me to help out, Mike can pass it to me. If Jammer stays on me, Mike can take the shot. So what happened? Mike goes into his move, Jammer jumps out, and Mike takes the shot anyway!

It wasn't a total disaster, but only because we got lucky. There was a scramble for the ball after the block, and I came up with it. Deuce was clapping his hands for the ball, yelling, "Reset! Reset!"

I just looked at him like *you must be trippin'*. I was one-on-one with Jammer, so I brought out one of my best moves. I gave him a quick first step with my right foot and ducked my shoulder, like I was going to try to get by him. He took a quick step back like he believed me. Then I went up as high as I could for a jumper.

He was off-balance and in a bad position to jump, but he did anyway. Now it was my shot that cleared his fingers by a centimeter. Mine didn't rattle in, though.

"Make a wish," I said as we watched the ball arc through the air.

"Hear the swish," I added as it dropped cleanly.

He gave me a nod and headed up the court. It was just 2–1, but four plays in, I think we both knew how this was going to go. His team was feeding him the ball at every opportunity. My team was treating the ball the way wolves treat meat: everyone fighting for it. His team was drawing the defense and dishing, and mine was just drawing the defense.

"Workin' nine to five," said Jammer as his team went up, 9–5.

They were two points away from being tourney champs, and we were two points away from being tourney chumps. As we ran down the court, I just went ahead and said it: "I'm the best player on this team. You've got to get me the ball!"

I'd never said that to them before. I think Mike and Deuce both knew it, and we boasted and talked trash all

the time. But no one had ever just flat-out said it like that. A weird look flashed across Deuce's face, and he nearly lost his dribble.

He didn't lose his dribble, but we definitely lost the game. Jammer's team won 11–7. He'd scored eight of his team's points, and I'd scored five of my team's. They celebrated at midcourt and soaked up some cheers from the crowd. We walked off the court shaking our heads.

I spotted Junior and headed his way. The first thing he said to me was: "Behind you, STAT."

I turned around and Jammer was right there. He looked really serious, and I had no idea what he wanted. But then he smiled and extended his hand. "Good game, man," he said. "You got some skills."

"Thanks. You can fly," I said. "Sure flew over us."

He shrugged and looked around. "I had a little more help than you," he said, quiet enough that only we could hear. Now it was my turn to shrug.

"Anyway, I like that 'make a wish' thing," he said. "You come up with that?"

"Yeah," I said, "on the spot."

"Mind if I steal it?"

"Nah," I said, and now I broke into a smile. "Wouldn't be the first thing you stole from me today."

He laughed. It was too soon after a tough loss for me to manage one of those, but I kept smiling.

"See you around, Amar'e," he said.

"I'll get you next time," I said.

"We'll see about that," he said, and turned to head back to his teammates.

Junior told me I'd played a good game and to keep my head up and, well, all the stuff you'd expect a big brother to say.

"Trophy presentation in five," said the guy with the clipboard.

"Cool," I said, searching for Deuce and Mike.

They were on the edge of the court talking to Dougie. As I walked over, I got the weird feeling that they might not want me there right now. It was weird. Back when we were just shooting around and playing for fun on our neighborhood court, it didn't matter if I was a little taller, a little better. But it was getting pretty hard to ignore at these tournaments.

"Hey, there he is!" said Dougie when he saw me.

He had a big smile and I got the handshake right this time.

"Good game, Amar'e," he said.

"Thanks," I said.

"Yeah," said Mike. "You had some nice moves."

That kind of surprised me. I thought maybe he'd still be upset about not getting the ball as much as he wanted today. And maybe he was, but it was cool of him to say that, either way.

"Definitely did your part," said Deuce with a little shrug.

That was cool, too. It reminded me of how we were walking around together like we owned the place before the game started.

"We all played hard," I said. "All day."

"Yeah," said Deuce. "We'll do better next time."

"When's that next tourney, again?" said Mike.

"The fourteenth," said Deuce. He turned to me: "You're in, right?"

It caught me off guard. The fourteenth was next Saturday. Before I really had a chance to think about it

I heard myself saying: "Sure. Okay. We're gonna win that one."

The guy with the clipboard was back. "Trophy time, guys," he said, pointing to the court. There was a little table set up with some paper streamers and stuff like that. On top, there were three trophies, each one larger than the one before it.

"I guess ours is the one in the middle," said Mike as we headed toward the table.

"The Mama Bear," I said.

Big Man and the shoelace twins were headed for the table, too. I was glad they won the third-place game. We said hi to them, and then stood around waiting for Jammer and his crew to make their way to the court. They were busy being congratulated by just about everyone. Finally they appeared. They collected a few last high fives at the edge of the court and jogged out to us.

The guy who'd been sitting at the scorer's table started speaking into a microphone. He said a lot of nice things, about the organizers and volunteers and teams and "outstanding young athletes." I guess they'd raised a bunch of money for charity, which was cool. Then he started handing out the trophies. He had some nice things to say to us, too. I appreciated it, but basically what it came down to was this: better luck next time.

"It's pretty nice, though," I said as we walked off the court with our Mama Bear trophy.

"Definitely the nicest one yet," said Mike, who was holding it. "Here, you carry it," he said to Deuce. "It'll look bigger that way!"

Mike and I started laughing. Deuce, not so much.

"Yeah, ha-ha-ha," he said. "Our next one will look bigger because it will have a big 'First Place' on the top."

"Great, we'll hold you up so you can see it!" I said.

Even he laughed at that one.

"Seriously, though," he said. "We've got to get some good practices in before the fourteenth."

"Maybe we can get Dougie to go, so we can run some two-on-two again," said Mike.

That was a good idea, but someone called my name before I could say so.

"Yo, Amar'e," I heard.

I thought maybe Dad had showed up a little late, but when I looked up, it was Overtime.

"Whoa," said Deuce. "He knows your name?"

"Guess so," I said, trying not to smile too wide.

I jogged over to where he was standing.

"Overtime, uh, Mr. Tanner," I said. "It's really an honor to meet you."

"You can call me Omar," he said, smiling.

I wasn't sure I could. I'd been raised on *sirs* and *ma'ams*, *misters* and *misses*.

"Sorry about the, well, the score," I said.

"You did your part," he said.

"Thanks, that's what people keep saying."

"Doesn't sound like you believe 'em."

I thought about that for a second. "I guess I just don't like to lose," I said.

"Neither did I," he said.

That made me feel a little better.

"Listen," he said, "I have a tournament of my own every year. It's invitation-only, and this is the part where I invite you."

He handed me a postcard. It had a sweet photo of

Overtime, back in his prime, soaring through the air for a monster jam. Underneath it said: *Fifth Annual Overtime Invitational: Florida's Best, Put to the Test!*

Wow, I thought. Actually, I might have said it out loud.

"You interested?" said Overtime.

"Of course," I said, still looking at the slick-looking card. I turned it over and there was an address in Polk County and some other information. "Absolutely!"

I turned the card back over and looked at his picture one more time. Then I flipped it back again. "Oh, wait," I said, reading a little more. "What about my team?"

"Well, like I said, it's invitation-only," he said. "But one of the guys I invited has already asked about you."

"Really?" I said. "Who?"

He pointed back out to the court. Jammer was still standing next to the table. He wasn't holding a trophy over his head like the last time I saw him. He had something else in his hand: the same postcard I had in mine.

"Whoa," I said.

Overtime gave a little laugh. "All right, I'll see you there, Amar'e," he said. "It was real nice to meet you."

"Yeah," I said. "Yes, sir. And thanks!"

My smile was so wide as he walked away that I felt it pushing my ears higher on my head. If I was going to be on the same court as Jammer again, I was glad it would be as his teammate. And it was cool to know he felt the same way.

Then I finished reading the card, and my ears fell right back to where they started. When I heard sneakers slapping the ground behind me, I slipped the card in my pocket and turned around.

"What did he say?" said Deuce.

"Yeah, what?" said Mike.

"He said, uh, it was nice to meet me," I said.

"Really?" said Deuce. "Wow."

"Cool," said Mike.

And it was true: He did say that. It wasn't all he said, of course, but I wasn't sure how to tell them about that part yet. I wasn't even sure what I was going to do about it. I just kept picturing the last line on the back of the card. It was the date of the invitational: *Join us on the 14th.*

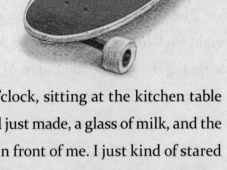

CHAPTER 9

I was home by four o'clock, sitting at the kitchen table with a big sandwich I'd just made, a glass of milk, and the postcard on the table in front of me. I just kind of stared at it as I ate, like I was expecting the little picture of Over-time to jump right out of the card and onto the table.

I wished it would. At least then I'd have someone to talk to about this. I had big news and no one to share it with. Dad was still at work. As busy as he was right now, he'd probably work until it got dark out. Junior had dropped me off on his way back to his own job. He was working a night shift for the guy who covered his day shift. Normally with news this big, I'd talk to Deuce or Mike. Not this time. Obviously.

I finished my sandwich, finished my milk, and looked at the card. There was someone I could talk to. I walked over and picked up the phone. I didn't have to look up the number. I knew it by heart. The phone rang once, twice, three times. Then someone picked up. It was my half brother.

"Hello?" he said.

"Hey, little man," I said.

We talked a little, and I told him about the tournament.

"Is the trophy really as tall as me?" he said.

Okay, so maybe I exaggerated a little.

"Nah, not really," I said. "But the next one will be. I'll send you a picture, okay?"

"Okay!" he said.

"Is Mom there?"

"Yeah, she's right here."

"Put her on, all right? Talk to you later, little big man."

I heard that weird bumping, rustling sound you always get when people are handing off the phone.

"Amar'e?" said Mom. "Hey, baby, it's good to hear your voice. How was the trip back?"

"Fine," I said. "Had a tournament today."

"How'd you do?" she said. "You have fun?"

"I had, um, some fun," I said.

"Mmm-hmmm," she said. She read me like a book.

"Yeah, not as much as the last one," I admitted. "But we won second place. Got a trophy."

"That's great!" she said. "And you know I'm not surprised. You know you're my superstar."

"Yeah," I said, looking down at my feet. I always felt a little awkward when she said stuff like that, even if she was, like, a thousand miles away. "And there's something else, too."

"Oh, yeah?"

"Yeah."

"You gonna tell me, or do I have to guess?"

"You know who Overtime Tanner is?"

"Oh, sure," she said. "He's a legend."

"I met him! He was really nice."

"That's great, baby! Were you at the superstars club together?"

"Aw, come on, Mom," I said, but I had to smile. "He invited me to his tournament."

"That's so great, Amar'e!"

"It's invitation-only. It says so right on the, well, the invitation."

"It *is* the superstars club!"

We laughed. I laughed maybe a little extra, because I was trying to figure out how to bring up the next part. I was trying to figure out how to tell her about the other tournament on the same day, about my friends.

"Is there something else, baby?" she said.

How did she know? She had magic mom powers or something. I wanted to tell her, but I still wasn't sure how to start. I hadn't even really had time to think it through myself.

"Nah," I said. "Just, I don't know, it's nice to talk to you."

"All right, baby. You know I'm always right here if you need to talk, right?"

"I know."

"All right, then, I better go. That little brother of yours is up to something in the other room. I can hear him out there."

"Okay," I said.

We said our *I love you*'s and hung up. And then it was just me in the kitchen again. I put the dishes in the sink and looked around. The house was as empty and quiet as it had ever been.

Until the next day anyway. Sundays were always a little extra sleepy. I didn't think Junior was working, but I knew he wasn't around. I'd even checked out back. Now I was just poking around the house. After all the excitement the day before, it was a big adjustment. I sort of felt like a microwave lasagna left out on the counter to cool.

I checked the freezer: no lasagna. Then I wandered into the living room. I was thinking maybe I'd watch some TV. When I went to pick up the remote, I saw something cool right next to it. It was a brand-new video game: *MechaNoize III: Cyborg Invasion*.

"Nice!" I said.

I didn't even realize this one was out yet. I turned over the brightly colored case to read the full description on the back and saw a little note stuck there. It was from Junior: *Let's do this!*

Cool! I put the game in and got right to it. It took me a few tries, but I finally cleared level 1. It was tough going, but I made those cyborgs pay for the trouble. How do you have guns for hands? That's got to make dinner awkward. I guess maybe cyborgs aren't big eaters.

Anyway, I finished level 1 and saved it. Then I got a new sticky note and a pen from the table by the phone. *Your turn!* I wrote and stuck it on the case.

It felt really good to get my mind off of the tournament situation.

CHAPTER 10

By the time practice started on Monday, I still hadn't told Mike and Deuce about the other tournament. It's not like I didn't have opportunities to, but every time I almost brought it up, my heart got faster and my mouth got drier. It made me nervous, and I just couldn't figure out exactly how to let them know. We'd recapped the action at the lunch table and a few other places for kids who hadn't been there. We might have concentrated a little more on the high points. And it's possible that Deuce claimed that Jammer was "like, sixteen or some-thing," but we mostly stuck to the facts. I didn't brag about how we were going to win it all this time, but I definitely didn't disagree either.

Now we were warming up on our local court. I figured maybe I'd tell them before practice really started, but I didn't. I got this crazy idea that maybe I wouldn't have to. If anything came up before the game, I'd be off the hook.

"Saturday still good for both of you?" I asked.

"Yep," they both said.

It was worth a shot. And it was only Monday. Something could still come up: a relative in town, the flu, a dentist appointment, a relative who was a dentist with the flu . . . I wasn't picky.

We talked about school a little and then eased into working on some plays. It was just simple stuff, and nothing with any contact. It was our first time on the court since Saturday, and it felt like we were all being extra careful. I guess we just remembered the hard feelings last time.

"That baseline play worked really well," said Deuce.

So we worked on baseline stuff for a while. Then we did some fast-break drills. We were warmed up by now, and things started to get a little more serious. In the drill we were doing, two of us had the ball, and the third guy was defending. There were only two other rules: You had to go fast, and you couldn't go backward. The goal was to get the defender to commit to one guy, so the other guy could get an easy layup.

So obviously you needed to pass, or at least make the defender think you were going to. But here's the thing: I was on defense on the first play, and I just knew Deuce wasn't going to pass the ball. When he gave a little head fake over toward Mike, I gave a little fake over in that direction. But I never left him. When he tried to speed past me, I was still right there. At his size, he couldn't go up over me. I basically engulfed him and snatched the shot right out of the air.

"Gotta pass that," I said.

He shot me a look. I thought he was going to say something, but he didn't. So two plays later, it was Deuce and me against Mike. I had the ball, and I shot toward the hoop. I had my head down, like I'd already decided to take it all the way to the rim. Mike jumped in front of me. As he did, I dished it off to Deuce for an easy score. I wanted to show him that I was willing to pass, that that's how we needed to play.

Instead he said: "See? If you'd done that more on Saturday, we could've won."

Now I was the one not saying what I was thinking: *No, because you couldn't beat your defender*. The next time it was Deuce and me, I did keep it. Mike jumped in front of me again, but he was too late. His feet weren't set and he was too deep under the basket anyway. I finger-rolled the ball up and in a split second before the collision.

Any good ref would call that a blocking foul on him. But there were no refs out here today, and Mike got up mad. "Take it easy, man!" he said.

"We've got to practice hard," I fired back, "or we'll never be as good!"

I didn't have to say as good as who. They knew who I meant.

So of course the next time Mike had the ball, he ran me over. I sort of knew it was coming, and I had good position and my feet set. It was a charge on him all the way, but again: no ref. He knew it, too.

"Charge," I said, peeling myself off the ground.

"Just trying to practice *hard*," he said.

Deuce gave him a low five and that really annoyed me. I even wondered if Deuce had passed it to Mike just so he could run me over.

"This drill isn't working," I said.

And it wasn't. It was like we were getting worse as a team instead of better.

"Yeah," said Deuce. "Because you're not doing it right."

"I'm the only one who *is* doing it right!"

"Then why am I the one who just scored?" said Mike.

"On my assist," said Deuce. "You're just mad because we schooled you."

I was mad. My face was hot and my heart was pounding, but it wasn't because they had schooled me. It was because they were teaming up on me and only seeing what they wanted to. If that's how they were going to be, I had something to show them.

"You really think that?" I said. "I can beat the both of you at once!"

"Yeah, right," said Deuce.

"Yeah," I said, looking straight at him. "Right."

"Okay," said Mike, puffing out his chest to try to make himself look bigger. "Let's go."

"I'm in," said Deuce. His chest was too small to inflate, but he squinted his eyes, trying to look tough. "What're we playing to?"

"One," I said. "That's all I need."

"Your funeral," said Deuce. "And we get the ball first."

I checked the ball in to him at the top of the key. Then I guarded Mike like Deuce wasn't even there. I knew that would get under his skin, and it did. He took off for the basket, and I took off a half second later.

We were both going full speed by the time Deuce reached the hoop. A pump fake or a pass back, and I was doomed. But I knew he was just going to go straight up with it. He was looking up at the hoop like it was a Thanksgiving turkey. I was taller and I jumped higher. The few steps he had on me weren't enough. When the shot went up, so did I. As I flew past, I plucked the ball right out of the air and came down with it like it was a rebound.

I took the ball back out, and started up the play. They both tried to guard me at once. I tried to zip past

Mike, since he was slower, but he just kept backing up and giving ground. As soon as I stopped or slowed down, I knew they were both going to swarm on me and tie me up. So I didn't stop.

I pushed hard, trying to turn the corner on Mike. I got close enough that Deuce had to come around the other side to seal me off. Then I spun back in the direction where Deuce had been and elevated. I had a clean twelve-foot shot, and I drained it.

"Game over." I looked at Deuce and Mike and walked off the court.

CHAPTER 11

I thought about that shot all the way home. I wasn't thinking about how I'd made it. I was thinking about why I'd had to. How had it become me against them? It felt like I was being double-teamed as soon as I stepped on the court.

Maybe it was time to let them know about the other tournament. Everything would be out in the open then — but maybe that would be even worse. I needed advice. But the house was empty again when I arrived. There was no one to talk to.

I walked into the living room. The *MechaNoize III* case was in the center of the table. I picked it up and saw the note Junior had stuck to the front: *Level 2 was ROUGH. You're up!*

I sat down and battled my way through level 3. It was definitely harder than level 1, but I was ready. I'd been battling for hours. I finished the level and saved it for Junior. I went over to the table by the phone to get another sticky note to leave for him.

Before I even got there, I realized I needed the phone more than the note. I dialed the number by heart.

"Hello?" I heard.

"Hi, Mom."

"Hi, baby," said Mom.

"Hi," I said. "You busy?"

"You know I always have time for you."

"Yeah," I said. I couldn't help but smile. Talking to Mom on the phone always kind of turned me back into a little kid, but I didn't mind. There was no one around to see me anyway.

"So what's going on?" she said. "Is something bothering you?"

She always knew why I was calling — sometimes even before I did!

"Yeah," I said. "It's" — I tried to think of how to start — "it's complicated."

"Well, I'm sitting, and your dad is paying the phone bill," she said with a chuckle. "So we've got time."

Her good mood helped me loosen up.

"It's my boys Mike and Deuce," I said. "You remember them?"

"Oh, sure," said Mom. "Your friends. I always liked those two."

"Yeah," I said. "They're great guys. It's just, well . . ." I kind of paused. But then I decided I'd just tell her. I hadn't called long-distance just to give her hints. "They're great guys, but they're maybe not quite as great as basketball players."

"Oh," said Mom. "Trouble on the court. I saw you and your brothers out there when you were up here. After I got done with the food shopping and came to pick you up. I could tell you were more serious about it."

"We all are," I said. "We're all more serious. We've even been practicing."

"And Junior tells me you've been doing real well in the tournaments," she said.

"Yeah, but . . ."

"But what, baby?"

"But I guess that's when things started to change, you know? We all get along fine off the court. But on the court, it's like one part basketball, two parts drama."

"Mmm-hmm," said Mom. "Those two go together sometimes."

"It's like we used to just play, and that was easy," I said. "But now we practice, and that's harder. And at the end of all that practice, we've got these tournaments. And they're great, but they change things. Once it's official, we have to worry about things we didn't have to worry about before."

"What kind of things?"

"Like, well, like who gets the ball the most."

"And who gets the ball the most?"

I paused again. "Me," I said. "Last time anyway. But it was just so we could win. That's the other thing, Mom. I'm not bragging or anything. . . ."

"I know you're not, baby."

"But I'm a little better than Mike and Deuce now. Like, Deuce is still really small. He used to be the fastest kid around, but at these tournaments . . ."

"He's not the fastest kid anymore," she said. I was really glad she understood. I mean, she was my mom, so she was going to have my back anyway. But I was glad someone else knew what was going on.

"So if we want to score . . . ," I started.

"Sometimes you've got to do the scoring," she finished.

"Yep."

"And maybe their feelings get a little hurt."

"I guess. Or maybe they hog the ball the next game. And run me over in practice."

"Because their feelings are hurt," she said.

"Oh, yeah," I said. I guess I hadn't really thought of it that way. We were both quiet for a second as I let that sink in.

"But it's weird," I said. "Because I still like them. And I still like the tournaments."

"It's just getting harder to like them both at the same time," she said.

"Exactly."

"And there's something else, isn't there?" she said.

How did she know?

"Man, Mom, you can read minds," I said.

"That's just called being a mom," she said.

"Well, you're right anyway. There's another tournament, a big one, and it's the same time as the next one with Mike and Deuce. And I, well, I kind of agreed to play in both of them."

"Oh, Amar'e," she said, like I was a puppy that kept chewing up her slippers. "This big tournament is the one you told me about last time?"

"Yeah," I said. I'd only told her the basics then, so now I told her the rest. I told her all about what Overtime had said to me. I told her about how good Jammer was, and that he wanted me on his team. I told her how this one would mean playing on a whole new level.

"Overtime invited me personally," I said, though I guess I'd already told her that.

"And Mike and Deuce?" she said.

"Nope," I said.

"So you could play in this invitational, and take a big

step forward," she said. "Or you could play in another little tournament with your friends."

"Yep, that's basically it."

"And if you play with your friends, do you think things will get better between you guys?"

"Probably not," I admitted. "They'll probably get their feelings hurt again. And I'll probably be mad about missing Overtime's tourney."

Now that I'd talked the whole thing out, it seemed a lot clearer.

"You know what I think?" said Mom.

"I think I know what you think," I said.

"Well, that's a lot of thinks," she said. "So I'll just go ahead and tell you."

"Okay."

"I think you're growing up, baby," she said. "And not everyone grows as fast or as far, not in school, not in life, and definitely not on the basketball court."

I thought about how Deuce and I were on the honor roll, but that wasn't really Mike's thing. Sometimes he busted on us for being nerds, but he never got in the way when we needed to study.

"Well, you've got to let yourself grow," she continued. "Think about three trees in a lot, and one tree is growing a little faster than the others. Can that tree crouch down and pretend they're all still the same size?"

"No, 'course not," I said.

"Well, that's you right now," said Mom. "You've got to let yourself be your best. And even if it's a little difficult right now, your friends are going to have to give you the space you need to grow."

She was right.

"Thanks, Mom," I said. "You're the best."

"Anytime, baby," she said.

I knew what I needed to do. But that didn't mean it was going to be easy.

CHAPTER 12

I was pretty jittery in school on Tuesday morning. I had this habit of chewing on my pencil when I was nervous, like before a big test or something. Well, if I chewed on it any harder now, it was going to become a second breakfast. I'd made up my mind, but now I had to tell Mike and Deuce. I just didn't know how to do it.

"So, uh, you ever think that we're all, like, trees?" I started.

We were in the hall, on our way back from art class. My palms were sweating, and I was sort of stumbling over my words.

"What are you talking about?" said Mike.

"We're all trees?" said Deuce. "I think you might have gotten too many paint fumes in art class."

"Leaf me alone!" I said, playing it off like a joke. They laughed a little and we headed to our next class. Fail. I tried again afterward.

"You guys heard about invitationals?" I said.

"Oh, sure," said Deuce. "Those are big-time. Aren't too many for kids our age. But that's basically how they spot the really top talent, like in high school and stuff."

"Yeah," said Mike. "Sometimes they even have full camps before the game. They get all the best guys."

This was off to a better start than last time, but I had to tell them now. If I let it drop again, it would be even harder to work up to it again. A little wave of nerves broke over top of me, but I pushed ahead.

"Well, I got invited to one," I said.

"Yeah, right," said Mike with a little laugh.

Not Deuce. He looked me right in the eyes. Once he saw my expression, he knew I was serious. He knew something was up, too, but he hadn't figured out that part yet.

"That's awesome, man," he said. His voice was sort of cautious. "Who invited you?"

"Overtime," I said, quieter than I meant to.

"Did you say 'Overtime'?" said Deuce. "Overtime Tanner invited you to play in a tournament?"

"Wait," said Mike, "you're serious?"

"Yeah," I said, trying to answer them both at once. "In his tournament: the Overtime Invitational."

"Wow, STAT, that's —" Mike started, but Deuce cut him off. He'd figured it out.

"When is it?" he said.

"Yeah, that's kind of the thing," I said. "I was gonna tell you. . . ."

"When?" said Mike.

"It's Saturday," I said. "The fourteenth."

Mike got that look on his face, like when he's trying to do math in class: "But that's . . ."

"The same day as our tournament," said Deuce.

"How can you play in both?" said Mike.

"I can't," I admitted. "Listen, guys, I feel really bad, but I've got to do this."

"But you already said you'd play in the one with us," said Mike.

Deuce didn't say anything. He just watched me like he did when he was defending me on the court and trying to figure out my next move.

"I told Overtime the same thing," I said. "It all happened really fast. I was sort of caught off guard."

Deuce shook his head.

"Come on, D," I said. "This is a really big opportunity for me."

"Yeah, for you," said Deuce. He looked over at Mike and said, "I guess our invitations got lost in the mail."

"Seriously," said Mike.

"Come on, guys," I said.

"I guess that's why you were hogging the ball so much at the tournament," said Deuce.

"What? No, that's not fair," I said.

"A lot of things aren't fair right now," he said.

I couldn't argue with that. Then the warning bell went off, and you can't argue with that either. We hustled to class.

• • •

We sat at our normal table during lunch. I wanted to make my case a little better. I'd spent most of that last class thinking about what I was going to say, but they didn't even want to talk about it. We basically wound up just sitting around chewing our soggy pizza squares and listening to Marcus tell his usual stories.

We didn't even sit together the next day. I sat down next to Tavoris and Marcus, as usual. Dougie sat down next. We all kind of scooted over to make room when Mike and Deuce appeared, but they just kept walking.

"Heard you guys are having an argument about hoops," said Tavoris.

"Yeah," I said. "That's about right."

"Oh, yeah?" said Marcus.

"Yeah," I said. "It's just kind of a dumb thing."

"Like a misunderstanding?" said Marcus.

"Yeah," I said. "Basically."

I left it at that. If I said anything more, Marcus would end up telling the whole class. He was a good guy, but asking him to stop flapping his gums was like asking a fish to stop swimming.

"I'm gonna go see what's up," said Dougie.

We watched as he walked over to their new table. He didn't come back. The rest of the day went pretty much the same. Right before the end of the day, word got back to me: Mike and Deuce were telling kids I was "big-timing" them.

I didn't think it was fair. It was just one tournament, and it's not like the last one had gone so great. And they both would've done the same thing if they were in my sneakers. I could think of a dozen reasons why it wasn't true. But it still stung. Big time.

CHAPTER 13

So, yeah, I was feeling a little hung out to dry when I got home from school on Wednesday. I went straight for the living room. My big brother and I had reached the final level of our video game. I fired up the game and got comfortable: The final level was always superhard on games like these, especially alone.

I started out carefully, scouting out my surroundings on the new level. I knew there was an ambush coming, but I didn't know where or when. I guess I must've been really concentrating because I didn't even hear when someone else came into the room. Then Junior crashed down on the couch next to me!

"Hey, STAT!" he said.

"Aaaah!" I said, pausing the game and trying to act like he hadn't scared the heck out of me. "I thought you were a cyborg ambush!"

"Nah," said Junior. "I'm the reinforcements. Got your back when you're under attack!"

"Cool!" I said. "I could use some backup right now."

"What do you say we finish this last level together?"

We went back to where the game was saved and started the level over, this time with two players. It was easier this time because I didn't have to watch the whole screen myself. The action started to build. Junior blasted a drone out of the sky with his electric-bolt launcher. Then I turned a weird spinning robot into scrap metal with my laser.

"You've gotten good, little bro," said Junior.

"You too," I said. "Those lightning bolts are pretty fierce."

He vaporized a wall next to us with an electric bolt, just to show off. But when he did, the space behind it was crawling with angry cyborgs. We went to work, zapping and blasting. We'd both kind of mastered this game on our own, so now that we were together, we were an awesome team.

The action kind of slacked off toward the middle of the level. This was the part where we were supposed to find something for the end, like a clue or a piece of equipment. So we were sort of sifting through the wreckage and looking in boxes and behind doors. It gave us a little time to talk.

"Thanks, man," I said. "I wouldn't have gotten through that last part if you weren't here."

"Glad to help," said Junior. "This is cool."

"Yeah," I said. "It's nice to have someone else here, too."

With nothing shooting at us at the moment, Junior risked a quick look over.

"You kind of have the run of the house these days, huh?" he said.

We finally found what we were looking for. It was a crazy laser that shot three beams, each a different color. Junior swapped out his lightning gun for this new weapon and tested it out a little. Right away, we knew this thing was going to come in handy in the final battle. I walked my guy over and picked up the electric-bolt gun, but what I was really doing was thinking of how to answer that last question.

"It's like, I don't know. It's like sometimes I come home and I yell out, 'Hello?' Just to check, you know? And it's like it practically echoes. Sometimes this little place feels like the Grand Canyon or some big old cave."

"Yeah, I've been there, too," Junior said. "That's why I came home early."

"Yeah?" I said.

"Yeah," he said. "Dad's busy season won't last forever, so I can cut back my hours a little until it's over."

He paused, but it kind of seemed like he had something more to say, so I didn't answer right away.

"Don't tell anyone," he said after a few moments, "but I kind of miss you guys sometimes."

"Don't tell anyone," I said, "but I kind of miss you guys, too."

Right then, a huge space zombie filled the screen.

"Just don't miss this guy!" Junior called out, but I was already taking aim. We leveled our weapons and blasted that sucker!

We kicked it into cruise control after that, heading for the big final battle these games always had at the end. As we went along, I filled him in on what had been going on. He already knew about the Overtime Invitational, of course, but I told him about the other tourney, my talk with Mom, and the rest of it.

He was quiet for a while, and I was worried he didn't know what I was talking about. But he did. He knew exactly.

"I got some invitations like that when I was your age," he said. "Your age and a little older, I guess."

"Really?" I said.

He smiled: "How do you think I knew who Overtime was so quick?"

"You played in the Overtime Invitational?" I said. I was so surprised I took my eyes off the game. The only thing that saved me from being vaporized was that three-beamed laser of Junior's.

"No," he said. "I didn't go. My friends didn't get invitations. They weren't as big or as good, and they didn't want me to go without them."

"Wow," I said. Talk about hearing an echo.

"And the thing is, I let them talk me out of it." He was still smiling, but it had changed. It was kind of a sad smile. "I didn't go to that one or the ones after it. Pretty soon, the invitations stopped coming. Even today I still wonder what would've happened if I'd gone."

We finally reached the big battle. For a few minutes, the only sounds were explosions on the screen and the sound of our fingers pounding the controllers. When the virtual smoke cleared, we'd finished the final level and I knew I'd made the right decision.

"I'm definitely going," I said.

"You bet you are," he said. "I'll drive you there myself. But be careful. You've got to do your thing, but you don't want to hurt anyone along the way. Those guys who talked me out of going? I might have some regrets, but they're still my friends. They're still some of my best friends."

"Yeah," I said. "Mike and Deuce have been my friends since forever. And they're good guys."

"Yeah, that's the other half," he said, shaking his head. "I don't know, little bro. It's tough. If only it were as easy as this game . . ."

We watched a funny little scene, with two cyborgs doing a dance as part of the on-screen victory celebration. One of them got dizzy and fell down and we both laughed. And right then, I realized something.

"Maybe it *is* that easy," I said, putting my controller down and standing up. "Maybe that's exactly it."

"Huh?" said Junior, looking over at me.

"Thanks, man," I said. "I'll explain later. Right now, I gotta go!"

CHAPTER 14

I hopped on my bike like it was a rocket. You can't really burn rubber on a bike, but I at least warmed it up as I tore down the street. I was headed straight for the basketball court. Mike and Deuce were usually there on Wednesdays. But I wasn't sure how long they'd stay, and it was already hours since school had let out. I put my head down and pedaled hard.

I reached the little park and biked right up the walkway to the court. A few squirrels had to jump for their lives, but I made it to the court in no time. I was relieved to see my friends. From the looks on their faces, it didn't seem like the feeling was mutual.

"Well, look who's here," said Deuce, doing a little crossover dribble.

"I see him," said Mike, shooting a lazy jumper.

I leaned my bike against the fence. "Hey, guys," I said. "Just shootin' around?"

"Yep," said Deuce. "Doesn't make much sense to practice for a three-on-three tourney with only two players."

He'd been taking shots at me all week. And I'd been letting him because I felt bad. But it seemed ridiculous now. I just looked at him and kind of tilted my head, like, *Really?*

"So why you here anyway?" said Mike.

They were both listening. Deuce even picked up his dribble, waiting for my reply. I needed to say what I'd come here to say. I could give them a big speech, but it was so simple.

"So, you guys know Junior has a job after school, and I barely see him these days," I said.

"Okay, but I don't see what that's got to do with anything," said Deuce.

"Well, today he came home early and we finished up a video game together. It was cool."

Deuce started dribbling again. He wasn't talking, but the ball was saying, *Get to the point*. So I did.

"It reminded me of how much I like just hanging out with him. It reminded me that we're brothers, but we're boys, too."

"Sounds like a real nice moment," Deuce said. But he said it with a little smirk on his face like he didn't really mean it.

"Let him talk, D," said Mike. Mike and Junior were tight. They had that big-guy bond. Still, it was time to make my case.

"Well, that reminded me of how much fun it is to just hang out with you guys, too," I said. "I was sitting there just playing around with my bro, and I realized that the three of us don't really do that anymore."

Deuce picked up his dribble again. He wasn't smirking anymore. He had a look on his face like he was remembering something. I just needed to make sure he was remembering the right things.

"It's like we've gotten so caught up in winning these tournaments . . . ," I began.

"That we forgot to just play the game," said Mike. "Forgot to have fun."

"Exactly," I said. "I mean, I knew you guys would be here today because Wednesday is practice. But come on, practice? We used to be out here just about every day. Because we loved playing."

"Yeah," said Mike. "You guys remember, we used to just come out here and mess around and play hoops until the sun went down?"

"I remember," I said.

Now we both looked at Deuce.

"Yeah," he said. "I remember." And then he smiled. "I mean, it was only a few months ago."

We all smiled. It seemed amazing that we'd gotten so serious so quickly.

"I mean, I like the tournaments," I said. "But what I really like is hanging out and shooting some hoops with my friends. With you guys. It's why I started playing in the first place."

"Yeah," said Mike. "Absolutely."

"I've, uh, I've been kind of a jerk this week, huh?" said Deuce.

"You know what?" I said. "I remember a lot of things, but that part? I've already forgotten."

Deuce and I slapped our hands together, and we squeezed tight.

"All right, you two," said Mike. "Break it up before you hug."

We all laughed.

"What d'ya say we just have some fun out here?" I said. "Like we used to?"

CHAPTER 15

*T*he numbers were still a little weird. All those hurt feelings didn't feel far enough away to start banging into each other playing one-on-two or two-on-one. This whole week had been two-on-one! But it didn't seem like we should be practicing for a tournament we weren't going to either. I hit a crazy shot warming up, and that gave me an idea.

"Let's play Crazy Horse," I said.

"I don't know," said Deuce. "I loved that when I was, like, nine, but . . ."

"Come on," I said. "It's fun."

We used to love to play H-O-R-S-E, where you all have to make the same shot or you get a letter, but we called this Crazy Horse because all the shots had to be crazy or they didn't count. Plus, there were twice as many letters, so the games lasted longer.

"I'm in," said Mike. "I'm gonna whup you guys."

That challenge was enough for Deuce. "In your dreams!" he said. "I'll go first."

Right away, he went into his patented move.

"Oh, no!" I called out as soon as I saw him start spinning.

He spun fifteen times around to his left, then fifteen times to his right.

"I'm gonna lose my lunch just watching this!" said Mike. "Why'd we let him go first?"

"I forgot about this!" I said.

Deuce spun around thirty times total, all really fast. Then he stopped and launched a ten-foot jumper. It rattled around the rim and dropped in. Mike and I tried to match him, but we couldn't. By the time we'd spun around all those times, we were way too dizzy. My shot barely even hit the backboard!

"These little guys spin like tops!" said Mike.

Just like that, he and I both had C and Deuce was in

the lead. But it was a really good game after that because we all had things we did well. Deuce was a master of the quick moves. Mike spent so much time in the post that he could hit crazy shots in close. And I, well, I had some game myself.

But after a while, it wasn't even about who was going to win. It was just about trying the craziest shots we could think of. It was about having fun. Half an hour later, I already had C-R-A-Z and now I had to match Mike's shot. He'd hit a left-handed hook shot while hopping away from the hoop on his right foot. I was lucky to even get iron.

"You are now officially C-R-A-Z-Y!" said Mike.

"I think we all are," I said, cracking up.

Deuce had been surprising me with his shots all game. Now he said something that surprised me more: "Just don't try any of these at the Overtime Invitational."

"You serious, man?" I said. We still hadn't really talked about Saturday.

"Yeah," he said, shrugging his shoulders a little. "It would be crazy not to go to something like that. I guess I was a little mad when I thought you were big-timing us. But we're friends first. If we can still hang out and play hoops and have fun afterward, I don't mind you being a little big-time."

"So you won't be mad if I play in the invitational?" I said.

Now Mike spoke up. "Now that I really think about it," he said. "I think we'd be mad if you didn't."

I looked at both of them: Mike and Deuce, my best friends.

"You guys better give me some space right now," I said.

"Why's that?" said Deuce.

"'Cause otherwise I really will hug you," I said.

"Run for the hills!" cried Mike.

But none of us ran anywhere. It's impossible to run when you're laughing that hard.

"What about you guys?" I said after we'd finally gotten back to the game.

"I don't know," said Deuce. "Maybe we'll come watch you."

I thought about it. "Nah," I said. "I think I've got a better idea."

CHAPTER 16

Dad and Junior both took Saturday morning off to come watch the tournament.

"Thanks for coming," I said as the three of us rode along in the front of Dad's big truck. "I know you guys are really busy right now."

"Wouldn't miss this one for the world," said Dad. "Anyway, the extra guys I hired are good workers. They can keep things going for one day without the boss looking over their shoulders."

"And I'm just here to make sure you don't slack off," Junior said with a smile.

"Yeah, great," I said. "Why do I get the feeling I'm going to have two bosses looking over my shoulders?"

We kept joking around like that the whole ride. I was a little nervous about my first big-time tournament, and it helped me relax. Knowing that my dad and brother would be there to support me helped, too. Pretty soon we were pulling into the lot.

"Good luck, STAT," said Dad as I hopped down out of the truck.

"Go get 'em, little brother," said Junior. "And don't forget to have fun out there."

As Dad wheeled the truck around the lot, hunting for the perfect spot, I headed for the sign-in table.

"Can I help you?" said the man sitting at the table.

"He's one of the players," said a voice behind me.

I wheeled around. It was Overtime.

"You ready, Amar'e?" he said, extending his hand.

"As I'll ever be, Mr. Tanner," I said, extending mine.

His handshake was strong from a thousand one-handed jams.

"You still have some time before the game," he said. "I'd advise you to use it."

He nodded over to the court, where a bunch of

kids were already warming up. I signed in fast and headed straight over. Jammer was the only guy I recognized.

"Hey, man," I said.

"What's up?" he said.

"Amar'e, this is Khalid," he said, nodding toward a short, stocky kid next to him. "Khalid, this is Amar'e."

"Hey," I said. Khalid nodded.

"He may look like half a tree trunk," said Jammer. "But he's one of the best passers you'll ever see."

"Really?" I said. I couldn't help myself. This was our point guard? He was no taller than Deuce and not much thinner than Mike. Khalid laughed it off.

"I get that a lot," he said. "You'll see."

"Our coach is over there," said Jammer. "We're waiting on the last few guys to start running some plays."

Instead of a bunch of short three-on-three games, the Overtime Invitational was just one five-on-five game. It was forty minutes long: four ten-minute quarters with a halftime thrown in for us to catch our breath. Jammer, Khalid, and I headed over to our coach.

"You Amar'e?" he said when I arrived.

I nodded. I thought he'd introduce himself but he didn't. "Yes, Coach," I said.

"Okay, I'm lining you up at power forward," he said. "Jammer will be the center."

I looked over at Jammer. He had the height and the hops, but he was seriously mobile for a center. I guess Coach read my mind because he said, "We're going to be fast out there. They won't be able to match our speed."

We all looked over at the group of kids assembling on the other side of the court: the other team. Then I snuck another quick look at Khalid. His speed? Really?

The other players arrived: a shooting guard named Brandon, a small forward named Eddie, a swingman type named Max. Coach told Max that he'd be starting the game on the bench but subbing in plenty.

"Our seventh guy has the flu," said Coach. "So you'll all have plenty of playing time."

One sub and a forty-minute game? I was suddenly glad I'd been doing all that bike riding!

We started off working on some plays on our half of the court. Khalid was definitely quicker than he looked, but it was hard to tell. We were just running through things sort of three-quarter speed. I think Coach just wanted to see what each of us could do. I tried to stay focused, but I could hear the other team running plays, too. It was hard not to sneak looks over every now and then. We may have had a speed advantage, but they definitely had more size.

Which was more important? We were about to find out. A whistle blew three times at center court. It was time for the game to start!

• • •

It was weird not to be the one jumping on the opening tip. But considering what happened when I jumped against Jammer last time, I was happy to let him handle it. He won it cleanly and tipped the ball back to Khalid. Just like that, we were off and running.

"Speed! Speed! Speed!" called Coach, and Khalid didn't disappoint. I was trailing perfectly on the play. I wish I could say I planned it that way, but I just didn't realize how fast he really was. His stocky legs fired like pistons in a sports car. As the other team scrambled to close him off in the lane, he dropped it back to me. I had an open jumper just inside the free throw line, and I drained it.

"Way to go, STAT!" I heard my dad and brother cheer from the stands.

I pointed at Khalid as we headed back up court. He gave me a little nod that seemed to say *told you so*. I'm glad he was right, because the game was intense! The other team was a little bigger, but they were still fast. And we were a little quicker but still pretty big. Basically, both teams were stacked.

By halftime, the score was tied at thirty-six apiece. Jammer was high-man for our team with fourteen points, and I had ten. The other team had a deadly outside shooter named Jay who'd already poured in sixteen points. We knew we were in a battle. We had our hands on our knees, breathing deeply and listening to Coach. After he went over the *X*'s and *O*'s, he said: "We have twenty minutes to go, and I know you're tired. I want you to take a moment and think about everything it took for you to get here."

Most of the kids were probably thinking about all the practice hours they'd put in and all the sweat they'd poured out on their own courts. But I was thinking of something else. Because what I'd done to get here, I hadn't done alone. I was thinking about all the help I had along the way.

I thought about the sound of Mom's voice on the phone. I thought about Junior and I beating back about four thousand cyborgs. I thought about Mike and Deuce helping me get better and then stepping aside so I could be here today. I thought about Dad up in the stands during his busiest time of the year. . . .

"All right," said Coach. "You got twenty more minutes in you?"

After all that? You know I did! This guy was a pretty good coach — whatever his name was. We were all pumped up, but the second half was just as tight as the first. Both teams were getting to know each other better — and that went for the defense, too. Kids were switching off on picks and boxing out on rebounds. These guys were good.

But some were better than others. Khalid gave us a lead at the end of the third quarter with two sweet passes. Jammer set a screen for me on the first one. The instant I broke free on the other side, the ball basically hit me in the hands. One more strong dribble and I was at the hoop. I went up strong and laid it in.

Then Khalid fed Jammer the one place his defenders couldn't go: above the rim. He lobbed a soft shot put of a pass up in the general vicinity and Jammer tipped it home. The crowd had gotten pretty big by then, and pretty much every one of them cheered. We were up 52–48 with one quarter left to play.

But when the fourth quarter started, Jay made some highlights of his own. The other team's star sank a pair of threes, and we went from up four to down two in a heartbeat. It was back and forth after that. I guess we all knew it was going to go right down to the final buzzer.

Sure enough, the score was knotted at 65 as the clock hit thirty seconds to go. The other team had the ball and called time-out. We huddled on the sideline.

"You all know where the ball is going," said Coach.

We did. Everyone on the court — and in the stands, too — knew it was going to Jay. The question was how: a screen, motion, some fast passes around the outside? We were all looking at Brandon, our shooting guard. He'd been matched up with Jay all day.

"Amar'e!" I heard.

"Yeah, Coach?"

"I want you to take Jay. You've got more length than Brandon, and that might throw him off. Can you do it?"

I looked around. Jammer, Khalid, Coach, and even Brandon were looking at me. "Yeah," I said. "I'll be on him like Khalid on a buffet."

Even Coach laughed. Then I had to go out there and do it. Jay was moving all over the court. He was shifty and changed directions on a dime. I did everything I could to stay with him. I didn't have a chance to look at the shot clock, but I knew it was winding down. He went outside a screen and I shot under it. When I picked him up again on the other side, he had the ball.

GULP.

He went right up with it. We both did. He got off the ground fast. I'd never guarded a shooter this good before, so I pretended it was a jump ball. I got up as high as I could with my hand straight up above my head. He released the ball. I extended my fingers.

TICK.

I got a little piece of the ball, just with my fingertips. I whipped my head around to see if it was enough.

"Short!" called Khalid, but Jammer was already on it. The ball hit the front rim and skipped down into his waiting hands. He tossed it to Khalid as we all turned and ran up the court.

I finally had a chance to check the clock. The shot clock was off because there were only fifteen seconds to go in the game. Time for one last push. They double-teamed Khalid at the top of the key with ten seconds left. He had to give up the ball. Eight seconds left. He passed it to me, but it didn't stay in my hands long. The last thing I'd seen before I got the ball was Jammer. He nodded at me. I knew where he was going.

The defense was closing in on me. Five seconds left. I fired the ball up toward the basket. It was a soft shot, and a little too high. But that's okay, because it wasn't really a shot. Two seconds left. Jammer's hands emerged above the rim and wrapped around the ball. One second left. And slammed it home!

The clock hit zero before he even landed. An air horn sounded, but you could barely hear it over the sound of the cheering crowd. Final score: 67–65. We won!

CHAPTER 17

It was pretty crazy right after the game. "Wait, wait," called Khalid over the noise. "Did someone say something about a buffet?"

The whole team laughed at that. Now I knew why I liked that guy so much: He reminded me of Mike. After that, we shook hands with the other team. We meant it, too. It was a good, clean — and very close! — game.

Jammer was ahead of me in the line. When we reached the end, he turned around. I held out my hand, but he shook his head.

"Nah, nah," he said. "Up top."

He held his hand all the way up, and I reached up and slapped it.

"You know what I mean, Amar'e? We'll both be playing up there pretty soon."

I nodded. "I'm almost there," I said.

"Next time I'll be lobbing it to you."

"I can't wait," I said. "But right now, I've got to go!"

"Yeah?" he said, surprised. "There's gonna be a big presentation. I caught a look at the trophies earlier. They're pretty sweet. You should stick around."

"Can't," I said. "Got someplace to be."

I headed toward the edge of the court.

"Where you going?" I heard someone shout.

It was Khalid. His eyes didn't miss anything. I didn't have time to explain, but I had something I wanted to say to him. "You made a believer out of me!" I called back.

"Not just you!" he said, nodding toward the crowd as it spilled out of the stands.

I wished I had time to talk to him some more. Instead, I pointed at him the way you point at a guy after he sets you up with a perfect pass. I figured Khalid had seen that move plenty.

I stepped off the court just as Overtime was stepping onto it. "You're heading the wrong way," he said.

"Kind of in a hurry," I said. "Sorry."

"Don't apologize to me," he said. "Not after the game you just played."

"Thanks," I said. "And thanks for the invitation. This was amazing."

"There'll be more of these in your future," he said. "And I'll make sure you get your trophy. Now get wherever you need to go!"

People started congratulating me as soon as I stepped off the court. I won't lie: It was pretty amazing. But I just said thanks and kept moving until I found Dad and Junior.

"Great game!" said Junior.

"Way to stand tall, STAT!" said Dad.

"Thanks," I said. "But can I get a ride? Like, right now?"

"Where's the fire?" said Dad.

"I think I know," said Junior.

Dad tossed him the keys to his truck. "Then you take him," he said. "Think I'm going to stick around a while.

Get a hot dog and maybe brag on my son a little. Just pick me up when you're done."

It was cool to see Dad enjoying his day off, but Junior and I were off and running. Well, jogging anyway. We reached the truck just in time to beat most of the traffic out of the parking lot. We left the tournament and headed for the highway. Twenty minutes later, we pulled into the parking lot of another, smaller tournament.

I hopped down out of the truck and headed for the entrance. Once I got inside, I spotted a familiar face. It was Deuce's cousin.

"Hey, Timmy," I said. "I'm not too late, am I?"

"Nah," he said. "They're just about to tip-off in the final."

"Awesome!"

We headed up into the stands. From our seats we had a good view of the team we came to see. I stood up and put my hands around my mouth. "Let's go, Mike!" I shouted.

"Let's go, Deuuuuce!" shouted Timmy.

We called out the last one together: "Let's go, Doug-EEEEEEEE!"

It hadn't been too hard to talk Dougie into taking my place for this one. Especially after I promised to help him get up to speed in practice.

"Think they heard us?" asked Timmy, as the ref tossed the ball up in the air.

Mike jumped straight up after it. He had springs in his feet and a smile on his face.

"Oh, yeah," I said. "They know we're here for them."